Bret Harte, Frank Holcomb Mason

The Life and Public Service of James A. Garfield

A Biographical Sketch

Bret Harte, Frank Holcomb Mason

The Life and Public Service of James A. Garfield
A Biographical Sketch

ISBN/EAN: 9783337010911

Printed in Europe, USA, Canada, Australia, Japan

Cover: Foto ©Raphael Reischuk / pixelio.de

More available books at **www.hansebooks.com**

THE

LIFE AND PUBLIC SERVICES

OF

JAMES A. GARFIELD

TWENTIETH PRESIDENT OF THE UNITED STATES

𝔄 𝔅𝔦𝔬𝔤𝔯𝔞𝔭𝔥𝔦𝔠𝔞𝔩 𝔖𝔨𝔢𝔱𝔠𝔥

BY

CAPTAIN F. H. MASON

LATE OF THE FORTY-SECOND REGIMENT, U.S.A.

WITH A PREFACE

BY

BRET HARTE

LONDON

TRÜBNER & CO., LUDGATE HILL

1881

PREFACE.

FEW words of mine can add anything to the story of the present First Magistrate of the United States as graphically told here. The Author has given his reason for telling that story in the fact that, until the first Tuesday in November, 1880, the life and name of the man who to-day takes his place among the potentates of the world, was doubtless unknown to the English public. But as it is equally true that the Author of General Garfield's history is still less known to an English audience than his hero, it is my wish to say briefly that, as friend, colleague, and compatriot of the Author of this book, I have known him as a gallant soldier, an earnest student, and

A

one of the first among American Western Journalists. No one could probably be more fitted for the work done here than the enthusiastic young student and staff officer of General Garfield; no one more qualified to tell the story than he who has modestly left his own personal record out of a struggle in which he was in the field a hero, and in Libby Prison a martyr.

BRET HARTE.

LONDON, 4th March, 1881.

CONTENTS.

———•———

A . 2

JAMES A. GARFIELD.

WHEN, on the 10th of June, 1880, it was known in Europe that the Republican National Convention at Chicago, after a week of extraordinary vicissitudes, had nominated as its candidate for President one of its own delegates, General James A. Garfield, of Ohio, there was apparent in the comments of the British and Continental press a tone of disappointment and surprise. It was more than suspected on this side of the Atlantic that the nomination had been a mere expedient, a make-shift suddenly adopted at a perilous moment to avert a rupture in the party; and that, as a result, it failed to fulfil the promise of a great occasion. So strongly had public opinion been impressed by the predominant

individuality of ex-President Grant, by the
brilliant statesmanship and magnetic personal
qualities of Senator Blaine, and the wonderful
financial record of Secretary Sherman, that when
the great Convention turned aside from all these
deserving aspirants and chose for the standard-
bearer of the party a man who, until the day of
his nomination, had hardly been mentioned as a
Presidential candidate, it naturally appeared to
those at a distance a weak and unfortunate compromise which might probably entail disaster.
But the Republican party throughout the United
States, that great political organization which
grew out of the instinctive loyalty of the people
to the cause of human freedom, and which has
never yet, in a crisis of grave responsibility,
made a false step, knew that the Convention
had made no mistake. It knew General Gar
field as the foremost statesman of his party in
Congress; a man whose speeches and whose
labours in important Committees of the House of

Representatives form a record of the most advanced and judicious legislation which has been accomplished at Washington during the past sixteen years. It knew him as a man who, born amidst the humblest surroundings, and having risen by his own unaided efforts to the Presidency of a College, a Major-Generalship in the Army, a seat in Congress and the Senate of the United States, as well as a leading position among the scholars and orators of his time, was an illustrious example of what energy and ability may accomplish under the stimulating influences of popular government and free institutions. That such a man should have been called to the Presidency of the Republic by the spontaneous and unsought votes of the people, was no accident, but a logical fulfilment of that intelligent principle which has so long prevailed in English politics—the crowning with highest honours of a leader who has become a dominant influence in his party. It was not only one of the most striking events in recent political history, but it is the normal and legitimate fruit of the civilization which has been ripened by a century of republican government in the New World.

It has been thought fitting, at the beginning of President Garfield's administration, to place before the European public—and particularly that of Great Britain, which is bound to the people of the United States by the strong ties of a common race and language—some record of the life of the New Executive, which may serve to impart a clearer understanding of the man who seems destined to be for some years to come a central figure in American politics. A man who, before the close of his fiftieth year, has become the chosen ruler of fifty millions of enlightened citizens, claims, by inherent right, the interest of intelligent people throughout the world.

It is the purpose of the present sketch to

present, in brief compass, the simple story of President Garfield's early struggles for education, his record as an instructor, his services as a soldier during the War of the Rebellion, and the salient points of his political career. Inevitably, such a narrative, however brief and imperfect, must involve, in order to become intelligible, some account of the political and military events in which he bore a part. There are also included in the text such short quotations from his speeches and published writings as may serve to illustrate his methods of thought and expression and define his attitude on leading questions of public policy. If to the impartial reader this account may seem to have somewhat the character of a eulogy, it is because the essential facts of President Garfield's life cannot be otherwise truthfully recorded.

I.

CHILDHOOD; SCHOOL AND COLLEGE LIFE.

JAMES ABRAM GARFIELD was born on the 19th
of November, 1831, in Orange Township,
Cuyahoga County, Ohio, about eighteen miles
from the present flourishing city of Cleveland. His father was of Massachusetts stock;
his mother was a native of New Hamp-
shire. The earliest record of his father's
ancestry is that of Edward Garfield, who, in
1635, was one of the proprietors of Watertown,
and was one of that select company of pure and
heroic men who came with Governor Winthrop
to find freedom of conscience amid the priva-
tions and hardships that beset the pioneers of
New England. It is believed that beyond
Edward Garfield the family was of Saxon
origin, a theory which is strongly sustained by
the fair complexion and purely German tem-

perament of President Garfield, who is not only
an enthusiastic lover of the language and the
literature of the Fatherland, but whose sturdy
thoroughness of method and tireless industry,
embodies the distinctive qualities of the German character.

However this may have been, his father and
mother, in January, 1830, settled in the Ohio
forest, where they purchased a tract of heavily
wooded land, built a small house of logs, and
began that struggle for life which, in a new
country, amid such surroundings, challenges and
develops in the pioneer the highest qualities of
fortitude and energy. Within three years
Abram Garfield had cleared the forest from a
portion of his land and begun the culture of the
soil. The woods adjacent to these new-made
fields were strewn with dry leaves and branches
which caught fire one summer day, and the
conflagration threatened to destroy the ripening
corn. The farmer was a man of remarkable

energy ; by tremendous exertion he threw up
a dyke of fresh earth between his fields and the
advancing fire, and thus saved his crops. Weary
and overheated by this violent labour, he became chilled while returning to the house, and
was seized with inflammation of the throat.
The medical treatment of that day was
uncertain, and too often accepted from the
hands of popular pretenders. The result
was a rapid development of the inflammation, and the intrepid pioneer, having walked
to the window and taken a last look at his
oxen, leaned against the head of his rude bed
and was choked to death, in the prime of his
life. . Before dying he consigned their four
children—of whom James was the youngest
—to the care of his wife, a woman who,
in all the qualities which combine to form an
intrepid, self-reliant Christian character, was fully
the equal of her husband.

The ensuing ten years were to the widow

Garfield and her four children a period of extraordinary struggles and privation. With a high, noble sense of her duties as a mother, she refused to send her older children out to work among her neighbours, but toiled and laboured to keep them together under her own eye and care. In some way the fields were ploughed and planted and the scanty harvests gathered. She made her children's clothing with her own hands, and performed a like service for the family of a neighbouring shoemaker, in return for which he made rude but substantial shoes for the little Garfields. During the winters, while the country was covered with snow, and all farm work except cutting wood and caring for the cattle necessarily suspended, the children, as soon as they were old enough, attended the neighbouring district school, and there, as well as from the teachings of his mother, the future President received his first taste of book-lore, which in later years was to inspire

him with the passionate ambition of scholarship.
From three years of age until ten the boy attended the daily sessions of that primitive
school.   Thenceforward, he was compelled
during part of each year to share somewhat in
the labour of the farm.   His poor mother could
provide him with but few books, but those he
read with an avidity that can hardly be described.
At the age of twelve he could recite from
memory almost the entire text of the " English
Reader," a book which was filled with selections
of prose and verse, and gave the young student
his first introduction to the standard writers of
his own language.

The profuse material which the latter years
of General Garfield's life offer to the biographer
compel us to pass rapidly over the period of his
boyhood ; a period which contained much that
was pathetic and suggestive.   He was from
childhood phenomenally precocious, both
physically and mentally.   When four years of

age he had received at the district school a copy of the New Testament as a prize for the best reader in the primary class. When eight years of age he had read all the books that his poor mother could provide, and began borrowing from the scanty libraries of the neighbours. " Robinson Crusoe," " Josephus," Goodrich's " History of the United States," and Pollock's " Course of Time," were successively read, and read again, until he could recite whole chapters of them from memory. He was particularly absorbed by two classes of books, those which related to wars and those which gave an account of adventures at sea. Meanwhile he had mastered arithmetic and English grammar ; had learned, in fact, all that the district school could teach him. He was robust and strong, and when elder boys were disposed to bully him by reason of his poverty, or the unprotected condition in which he was placed by his mother's widowhood, they met a prompt resentment and an ugly customer. His nautical readings gave him a spirit of valorous adventure, and, to the great distress of his Christian mother, he became what was known in the phrase of the neighbourhood as a " fighting boy."

At the age of sixteen he made a contract with his cousin to cut one hundred cords of wood for the sum of twenty-five dollars. The task was performed in a tract of high woodland which commanded a view of Lake Erie, upon whose blue waters he could see the steamers and sailing vessels entering and leaving the port of Cleveland. The sight revived and stimulated all his latent love of the sea, and he resolved to become a sailor.

After his work was completed, he walked to Cleveland, went on board a schooner lying at the wharf, saw a drunken, boisterous crew and a brutal captain, and was at once cured of his delusions concerning the romance of the forecastle. An hour afterward he chanced to meet another cousin who was proprietor of a canal boat plying on the Ohio and Pennsylvania Canal between Cleveland and Pittsburgh. He asked for employment, and was offered a situation as driver. From reefing a topsail, of which he had so often dreamed, to driving a tandem mule team on a towing-path, was a rude and sudden descent; but the young Viking had resolved to become a sailor, and he began as a canal driver, not because he had any liking for the business, but because it gave him employment by which money could be earned and something learned of navigation. He would take his first degree, he thought, on the canal, and then push for the blue sea and the ships that sail to distant lands.

Like President Lincoln, General Garfield is a man about whose early life people love to weave romances. The canal episode has been made to serve the same purpose in the recent Presidential campaign that Mr. Lincoln's rail-splitting did in that of 1860, and it has thereby become magnified greatly beyond its just proportions. It has been hastily assumed from the fact that James Garfield was once a canal driver, and punished a hulking loafer who sought to abuse him, that he was a boy of low tastes and quarrelsome temperament. Nothing could be more untrue than such a theory. His brief service on the canal was purely accidental, the temporary expedient of a boy who had to make his own way in the world, who wanted to go to sea, and caught at what seemed the obvious means of fulfilling his purpose. He is neither proud nor ashamed of it.

But Providence had other uses for the large-brained, aggressive boy than the rude life of a sailor. At the end of three months of canal driving he was carried to his mother's home in Orange, delirious with malarial fever. That illness gave his mother the opportunity for which she had prayed, and, during the five months of slow convalescence through which she nursed him back to health, she planted in his mind the seeds of a new and higher ambition, which helped to change the whole course of his life. When her books had all been read to him and her words of counsel exhausted, the schoolmaster was called in to add his scholarly advice. Thus persuaded, young James, on his recovery, went to the Geauga seminary, fourteen miles distant, and with but seventeen dollars in his pocket enrolled himself as a student, and began the study of Latin, Greek, and mathematics. After the first week he was easily the first pupil in every class to which he belonged, and from that moment there was no further danger to be feared from canal or sea. The thirst for knowledge took complete possession of him. He not only mastered his studies but read the library of the Academy almost entire, and resolved to attain the fullest education that a course of classical and scientific study could afford. This resolu-

tion once fixed, every obstacle was overcome.
During vacations he taught school, or worked
upon farms during the season of harvest.

While at the Geauga seminary he had embraced religion, and joined a sect known as the
" Disciples of Christ," the same who have been
otherwise called "Campbellites," from the
fact that Alexander Campbell, the eloquent
Scotch preacher, had been a prominent leader in
developing and extending the influence of that
church in the United States. The creed of the
" Disciples" is simply a belief in the New Testament, the divinity of Christ and his atonement,
in baptism by immersion, and, for the rest, "a
protest against imposing as a condition of church
membership any human formula of divine truth."

The " Disciples" were about that time making
great progress in Northern Ohio, and an academical school was established in the small village
of Hiram, thirty miles from Cleveland, in which
the future clergymen and elders of the church
were to be trained and educated for their work.

Young Garfield was naturally drawn to the new school, and came with his usual scant supply of money, but with an ambition and energy that overcame all difficulties.   He was the first scholar in all his classes, soon became tutor, and finally a teacher, while still pursuing his studies and enriching his mind with a wide and thorough course of collateral reading.   His proficiency in the Greek and Latin languages was phenomenal, and in a surprisingly short time he had reached a point in academical study which enabled him to enter the junior class of Williams College, one of the oldest and most advanced institutions of learning in New England.   The President of Williams College at that period was the venerable Mark Hopkins, one of the most accomplished teachers of his time ; a man of broad attainments, generous impulses, and that nameless, magnetic capacity which enables its possessor to inspire young men and develop their abilities without dwarfing their individuality.

President Hopkins measured the mental

calibre of the young Western giant at a glance,. and there sprang up between the teacher and his student a friendship which, since that day, has grown stronger and closer with the lapse of time. On the 17th of July last, a month after the nomination of General Garfield for President, the honoured ex-President of Williams, who has long retired from active duties, wrote to a friend a letter embodying the following estimate of young Garfield's college life :—" My first remark is, then, that General Garfield was not *sent* to college, *he came*. This often marks a difference between college students. . . . . A second remark is that the studies of General Garfield had breadth. And as General Garfield was broad in his scholarship, so was he in his sympathies. No one thought of him as a recluse, or as bookish. Not *given* to athletic sports, he was fond of them. There was a large general capacity applicable to any subject, and sound sense. As he was more mature than most, he naturally had a readier and firmer grasp of the higher studies. Hence his appointment to the metaphysical oration, then one of the high honours of the class. What he did was done with facility, and by honest and avowed work. There was no pretence of genius, or alternation of spasmodic effort and of rest, but a satisfactory accomplishment in all directions of what was undertaken. Hence there was a steady, healthful, onward, and upward progress, such as has characterized his course since his graduation. If that course should still be upward, it would add another to the grand illustrations we have already of the spirit of our free institutions. . . . ."

Professor Chadbourne, who knew Garfield intimately in the lecture hall and class room, and who has since succeeded President Hopkins as the head of the faculty of Williams College, says of him : " General Garfield graduated from Williams College in 1856. He evidently came to college for a purpose, and nothing turned him from that purpose. · He recognized the fact that the professors were placed over the college to instruct and govern the students. He gained from them all the good he could, and those now living remember him as a noble man even as a student. He then gave promise of what he has since become—that is, a man equal to any emergency, a man of strong convictions of duty and unflinching courage. Few can have the opportunities for the kind of success achieved by General Garfield, but had no political honour ever have come to him he would have been a power for good in the world."

During his two years of study at Williams, Mr. Garfield achieved distinction, not only by the brilliancy and thoroughness of his recitations, but through his readiness and eloquence as a debater and the breadth and ability of his essays upon serious topics, which were published in the *Williams' Quarterly Review.* A class-

mate says of him : " Garfield's greatness was to
our young eyes enigmatical, but it was real.
There was a good deal of him in body, soul, and
spirit." He graduated in 1856, winning the metaphysical oration, one of the highest honours in
an exceptionally able class. He returned to
Hiram, and at the opening of the academic
year resumed his labours as Professor of Ancient
Languages and English Literature in that
rapidly rising school. As a teacher he was un-
rivalled. Mr. Burke A. Hinsdale, who is now
the able President of Hiram College, writes of
Professor Garfield at this period : " His method
of conducting a recitation was his own, com-
bining the question that required a text-book
answer, the topic to be handled, the call for the
pupil's own opinion, and the teacher's discussion
of the matter in hand. As a drill master, many
teachers surpassed him ; but as an educator in
the best sense, he stood with the first. His
class-room glowed with life. Probably no pupil

remembers having spent in it a dull hour. While placing its proper valuation upon learning and information, his great aim was to awaken the faculties of the student. There is a process known to the laboratory as *energizing a magnet.* By passing electrical currents around a bar of common iron, the electrician gives the bar magnetic virtue. There is an analogous process known to the educator; the most important work that he can render the student is to *energize* him. Among the teachers whom I have known, Garfield stood alone as an energizer of young men and women. He revealed the world to the student, and the student to himself. He called out thought, set the faculties in full play, awakened courage, widened the field of mental vision, and poured in abundant measures of inspiration." His methods as a teacher were similar to those of the renowned Dr. Arnold of Rugby, for whom he cherished a reverent admiration, and "Tom Brown" was as much a part of a student's course of reading at Hiram College as " Thucydides" or the " Æneid."

After one year of service as teacher he was promoted to the Presidency of the Faculty. He was then twenty-six years of age, and had already become the controlling influence and inspiration of the school. No one of the three hundred students who formed the classes at that time will forget the rich privilege which they enjoyed in hearing the morning lectures of President Garfield in the chapel. There was first the assembly, then prayers and a chapter read from the Bible, and for the remainder of the morning-hour an extemporaneous address by the Principal. Sometimes it was upon a topic chosen from the lessons of the day; oftener it was upon some fresh event in politics, science, or literature. One morning he read the " Three Fishers" of Charles Kingsley, which had just appeared in an English magazine ; anon a new idyl by Tennyson would constitute an enchanting theme, and once the text was a newspaper paragraph relating the tragic fate of Hugh Miller, the lesson of whose noble life was set forth in words of eloquent and impressive eulogy.

Above all else, President Garfield developed among his students a spirit of manliness and self-reliance. He encouraged the boys in athletic exercises, often superintending personally their games of cricket and football, and naturally drew them to himself with a strength of personal devotion which amounted almost to idolatry. One of the ablest of them, who has since achieved conspicuous success as an educator, writes of his devotion to his mentor : "Then began to grow up in me an admiration and love for Professor Garfield which has never abated, and the like of which I have never known. A bow of recognition, or a single word from him, was to me an inspiration."

Besides his educational labours President

Garfield, during this period, attained eminence as a preacher. He was not ordained, but de-livered his powerful and convincing sermons from the pulpit with the consent and encourage-ment of the Church authorities. In the winter of 1859-60 he became involved in a public debate with a Spiritualistic lecturer, named Denton, who sought to overthrow the teachings of the Bible with the revelations of geology. The battle was fought over the development theory, which Darwin subsequently formulated in his doctrine of evolution. Garfield had but three days in which to prepare for the contest with an able opponent, who had his side of the subject carefully digested, and his facts and theories at his tongue's end. There was brief time in which to consult authorities, or glean through a library for scattered grains of proof, so the College President hit upon a character-istic expedient. Calling together half a dozen of his most advanced students, he laid before

them a skeleton of the argument that he proposed to develop in the debate.. He showed
them each point that he desired to establish,
then, assigning to each his task, he turned his
six young assistants into the College library to
seek out and copy, in condensed form, all proofs
and authorities bearing upon the vital points of
his argument. In twenty-four hours the work
was finished : a second meeting was held, in
which each of the auxiliaries brought forward
and added his contribution to the common fund.
Thus equipped, Garfield met and completely
overwhelmed his opponent, who, after that
defeat, abandoned his theory and gave up the
fight against the inspiration of the Bible.

It had. now become evident that Hiram
College, flourishing and useful as it had become,
could not long absorb the energies of its
Principal. The quality and capacities of his
mind led him resistlessly to wider and higher
fields of activity. The Free Soil political party,

which had grown up out of the question whether slavery should be established in the territories of Kansas and Nebraska, had assumed national proportions, and on the political horizon began to be heard the first mutterings of the storm which was finally to overwhelm the country with the fury of civil war. It is said, by those who knew Mr. Garfield as an undergraduate, that he manifested, during that period, little or no interest in politics. But in June, 1856, the Free Soil party, voicing the instinctive protest of the Northern States against the extension of slavery, adopted a platform embodying that principle, and nominated, as its candidate for president, General John C. Fremont, a man who had distinguished himself as an explorer of the mountainous country along the Pacific Coast of the United States. A month after the nomination of Fremont Garfield graduated from college, returned to Ohio, and, during the weeks that intervened before the resumption of his duties at

Hiram, he made a few campaign speeches in the
neighbouring townships and villages.   He was,
of course, a novice in political methods, but he
was full of enthusiasm for the cause of freedom ;
and the mature logic of his reasoning, and the
vigour and force of his language, foreshadowed
the greatness which he has since attained as a
political orator.   But the Democratic party, in
1856, was strong and united, and James
Buchanan was elected over Fremont as President by a decisive majority.   Buchanan was a
weak and nerveless President; he was completely
under control of the slave-holding Democrats of
the South, who, under his imbecile rule, sapped
the military and naval resources of the Government, and boldly matured their scheme of
secession from the Federal Union.   Meanwhile,
the spirit of resistance to this treasonable aggres-
sion was steadily growing stronger and more
earnest throughout the free States of the North.
Out of the elements which constituted the Free

Soil party of 1856, there was organized the National Republican party, which took the field in the memorable Presidential contest of 1860.

It was during those four critical years, in which the opposing forces which finally met on the battle-fields of the Rebellion were silently marshalling for the coming struggle, that President Garfield, of Hiram College, was drawn gradually into political affairs.   It was an ideal period for a man of his theories and temperament to enter public life.   The conscience of the people was awakening to the enormities of the slave system, and discerning men began to see and admit that the "irrepressible conflict" between slavery and freedom could have but one termination, the complete subjugation of one by the other. The Southern leaders, although supported by a minority of voters, possessed greater skill and audacity as politicians, and they were openly determined to maintain their control of the Government against the growing majority of the

North, or, failing in that, to withdraw the slave-
holding States from the Union and set up a
Confederacy in which the sacredness of slavery
should be recognized and its permanence
established for ever. In the discussion that
attended this transition state of public feeling,
President Garfield took an important and con-
stantly growing part. In the campaigns pre-
ceding the local State elections of 1857 and
1858, he made numerous speeches and attained
a recognized political influence in the north-
eastern part of Ohio. The Legislature of a
State consists, like the National Congress, of
a Senate and House of Representatives; and
in 1859, the Senatorial district in which
Hiram was located elected him a State-
Senator.

The Legislature assembled during the first
week of January, 1860. Senator Garfield was
then twenty-eight years old, by far the youngest
member of the Senate. But he was already a

polished and forcible speaker, he had clear and
well-defined opinions on all leading issues, and
he took, from the first, a high rank among his
colleagues. The Republican members were in
the majority in both branches of the Legislature,
but they disagreed on the whole series of questions growing out of the slavery dispute. The
Conservative Republicans advocated a policy
of compromise, and preferred to temporize with
an acknowledged and increasing menace rather
than risk an outbreak that might imperil the
Republic. The Radical Republicans, on the
other hand, insisted that the time for concession
and compromise was past, and that the con-
spiracies of slavery must be boldly met, and, if
possible, overthrown. At the head of the
Radical Republican wing of the Ohio Legislature during that momentous season were three
men, who became known as the "Radical
Triumvirate." They were Garfield, Senator
J. D. Cox (afterwards Governor of Ohio and

Secretary of the Interior in the Cabinet of President Grant), and Professor James Monroe, of Oberlin College, who has for many years since been a leading member of Congress from Ohio. Although these three men were firm and unyielding in their opinions, they were neither aggressive nor defiant. They dreaded and deprecated the storm which they knew to be rising, but not even the dread of war could swerve them from fidelity to their convictions.

The Legislature adjourned in April, a few weeks prior to the beginning of that fatal complication in national politics which precipitated the war. The Republican Convention at Chicago nominated, as its candidate for President, Abraham Lincoln, of Illinois. The Democratic Convention assembled at Charleston, South Carolina, and, after a protracted and acrimonious struggle between its Radical and Conservative elements, the Convention was split into two factions, each of which adopted a separate platform and nominated its own candidates for President and Vice-President. Thus fatally divided by internal dissensions growing out of slavery and the question of State rights, the Democratic party was defeated in detail ; Lincoln carried a plurality of votes as against either of the Democratic candidates, and the die was cast.

An American President is elected on the first Tuesday of November, but he does not assume the duties of his office until the 4th of the following March. During these intervening four months in 1860-61 the second session of the Ohio Legislature, of which General Garfield was a member, took place. That winter was an epoch in American history ; and the Legislature, carried away by the current of popular feeling, forgot all merely local legislation and plunged into the arena of national politics. The question of State rights was the grand issue. Can a sovereign State be coerced against its will by Federal authority? Can a State or Confederation of States. secede from the Union at will? Is the National Government superior to that of a sovereign State, and in general what are the rights and the obligations of a State to the Republic of which it is a part? These were among the various forms and phases into which was condensed the perilous question which was rapidly opening a chasm between the two sections of the Union which it would cost four terrible years of war to bridge.

The election of President Lincoln had been accepted by the leaders of the Pro-Slavery party as the signal for secession. They understood the meaning of his election to be that a minority of Southern senators and representatives was no longer to control the Government. They declared their purpose to withdraw the Southern States from the Union, and defied the vacilating administration of President Buchanan to prevent or punish their treasonable purpose. To every loyal person who understood the true meaning of the case, secession meant war; and the Legislature of Ohio, like those of other loyal States, began to take measures to meet the impending crisis. In January, 1861, a Bill was discussed in the Ohio Senate to provide for raising and equipping 6,000 militia, and in that debate Senator Garfield made a speech which thrilled the State at the time, and declared the position which he held until the close of the succeeding struggle. A single extract will reveal its character.

It was asserted by the opponents of the measure that such an enactment would have the character of coercion. Senator Garfield said: " If by coercion it is meant that the Federal Government shall declare and make war against a State, then I have yet to see any man, Democrat or Republican, who is a Coercionist. But if by the term it is meant that the General Government shall enforce the laws, by whomsoever violated, shall protect the property and flag of the Union, shall punish traitors to the Constitution, be they ten men or ten thousand, then I am a Coercionist. Every member of the Senate, by his vote on the eighth resolution, is a Coercionist ; nine-tenths of the people of Ohio are Coercionists. Every man is a Coercionist or a traitor."

The world knows what occurred at Washington during the winter of 1860–61. On the 4th of March President Lincoln was inaugurated. The Southern senators and representatives left their seats in Congress and went forth to frame a Confederacy, which, in the words of Alexander H. Stephens, its Vice-President, should have the divinely-ordained institution of slavery "as its chief corner-stone." The Southern States, with the exception of Kentucky and Missouri, passed ordinances of secession from the Union. Batteries were erected on the islands and shores of Charleston harbour, and in April opened fire upon Fort Sumter. It was found that Floyd, the Secretary of War in the Cabinet of Buchanan, had adroitly scattered the few regiments of regular troops which were then in service at remote stations, most of the arms and ammunition of the Government had been removed to Southern arsenals, and the new Administration was for the moment helpless. But the roar of the rebel batteries at Charleston roused the loyal heart of the nation and the drum-beat called a patriot people to arms.

II.

GENERAL GARFIELD AS A SOLDIER.

Hark ! I hear the tramp of thousands,
   And of armèd men the hum ;
Lo ! a nation's hosts have gathered
   Round the quick alarming drum—
      Saying, ' Come,
      Freemen, Come !
Ere your heritage be wasted,' said the quick
   alarming drum.

Bret Harte.

IT was inevitable that a man of Senator Garfield's courage and opinions should be found at
the front early in the great conflict. At first he
hoped, against his convictions, that Secretary
Seward's prediction might be fulfilled, and the
rebellion suppressed without a war to the death
but the disaster at Bull Run in July, 1861, ended
that momentary delusion, and the loyal States
began to gird themselves up for the supreme
struggle. Seven days after the battle of Bull Run,
Senator Garfield accepted an appointment as

Lieutenant-Colonel of a regiment then organiz-
ing at Camp Chase, a large camp of instruction
which had been opened near Columbus, the
capital of Ohio.. He reported promptly for duty,
and a few days later received a commission, as
Colonel, to organize and command a new regiment, the Forty-second Ohio Infantry. Within a
week a hundred students from Hiram College had
enlisted as a company in the new regiment. Other
volunteers poured into Camp Chase, and before
the 20th of August the regiment was filled to its
maximum number. The men were uniformed,
partly armed, and set to drilling, marching, and
studying the details of infantry tactics night and
day. But the busiest, most exhaustive student
in the Forty-second Regiment was its Colonel.
With his usual comprehensive thoroughness, he
mastered all that books could teach him of the art
of war. Not merely the manual of arms and the
formation of companies, battalions, and regiments,
were the subjects of his study ; but every detail

of equipment, camp discipline, military transportation, and the relative functions of Infantry, Cavalry, and Artillery, were learned, in theory at least, by the tireless Colonel. The commandant of the camp and the experienced officers attached to other commands were astonished to find the Colonel of the Forty-second always fully prepared for every new duty. He infused his own enthusiastic spirit into his men, and by protracting the hours of drill and exercise almost throughout the entire day, he rapidly hardened and trained them for the rough service of the field. He established a school for the regimental officers, over which he presided as instructor, and here again every minute detail of camp and picket duty, company and battalion tactics, even the cooking of rations in the field, was taught to the captains and lieutenants. At the end of three months of this work the Forty-second regiment was ordered to the front. Its men were as yet of course only recruits.

Not an officer or soldier in the regiment had ever
been under fire. They had the theory of infantry service well mastered, they had acquired a
fair proficiency in regimental tactics and the
manual of arms. Most of the men were, from previous experience, skilful marksmen; and, better
still, all were, as volunteers usually are, eager to
fight. The regiment was in all aspects up to
the best standard of the fifteen hundred thousand soldiers who wore the blue of the Union
Army during those four years of war. Its men
were indeed above the average of education and
intelligence, even in that army of enlightened
volunteers; but the regiment as a whole included
material sufficiently miscellaneous to make it
capable, when occasion required, of many varied
kinds of service. There were in the ranks under-
graduates of all grades, from freshman to senior;
there were lawyers, clergymen, teachers, car-
penters, blacksmiths, engineers, farmers, printers,
and machinists. They could build bridges, repair

and run locomotives, build houses, operate a
telegraph, or navigate a steamboat. When they
received their arms—long, heavy Belgian rifles,
which were loaded at the muzzle—the gunsmiths
in the ranks altered and perfected the " sights"
of their comrades' weapons until the Forty-
second could become a regiment of sharp-
shooters. It need hardly be said that material
of this kind, well officered, develops rapidly
amid actual warfare into capable and effective
soldiers.

The field of operation in the South was of
enormous extent; the army, during the first
two years of the war, was but imperfectly provided with many essential materials ; and the
Forty-second found, like other regiments, full
scope for all its varied capabilities.

The regiment left Columbus on the 14th of
December, and proceeded by rail to Cincinnati,
on the Ohio river. Beyond that stream lay the
State of Kentucky, not technically out of the

Union, but disloyal at heart, and invaded at that moment on its eastern frontier by a Confederate force of 5,000 men under Humphrey Marshall. Colonel Garfield was ordered in person to Louisville, to report to General Buell, the commanding officer of that department. The historian of the Forty-second Regiment says:—"On the evening of the 16th, Colonel Garfield reached Louisville, and sought General Buell at his head-quarters. He found a cold, silent, austere man, who asked a few direct questions, revealed nothing, and eyed the newcomer with a curious, searching expression, as though trying to look into the untried colonel, and divine whether he would succeed or fail. Taking a map, General Buell pointed out the position of Marshall's forces in Eastern Kentucky, marked the locations at which the Union troops in that district were posted, explained the nature of the country and its supplies, and then dismissed his visitor with the remark :

'If you were in command of the sub-depart-
ment of Eastern Kentucky, what would you
do? Come here to-morrow morning at nine
o'clock and tell me.' Colonel Garfield returned
to his hotel, procured a map of Kentucky, the
last Census Report, paper, pen, and ink, and sat
down to his task. He studied the roads,
resources, and population of every county in
Eastern Kentucky. At daylight he was still
at work, but at nine o'clock he was at General
Buell's head-quarters with a sketch of his
plans."

General Buell read the paper carefully, and
made it the basis of an immediate order organ-
izing a brigade of four regiments of infantry
and a battalion of cavalry, placing Colonel
Garfield in command, and ordering him to
Eastern Kentucky to expel Marshall's force
in his own way.

The campaign that followed must be related
in a paragraph. The force thus suddenly

placed under Colonel Garfield's command was distributed over a large area of mountainous and thinly-settled country ; the roads at that season of the year were almost impassable, and the enemy's troops were numerically superior to his own. Nevertheless, he vigorously set about his task, and on the 10th of January confronted Marshall's entire brigade in the valley of Middle Creek, a small tributary of the Big Sandy River, which flows into that stream about eighty miles above its point of confluence with the Ohio. Garfield's force had reached the battle-field by forced marches over mountain paths impracticable for waggons. Marshall had abandoned some entrenchments lower down the valley, and showed a disposition to retreat : Garfield was therefore obliged to strike him at the moment, without waiting for the last of his troops to assemble. With only 1400 men he forded a swollen creek, scaled a steep wooded hill, and attacked the enemy in a strong position. After a sharp fight of five hours, the victory of the assailants was complete; the Confederates were driven over the hill, and at nightfall retreated, leaving their dead unburied, and recrossed the Cumberland mountains into Virginia. It was the first substantial victory won by a Union force during the war. Its only pertinence to the purposes of this sketch is to illustrate, as such an event only can, the character of the untried soldier who planned and won the battle of Middle Creek, his instantaneous, unerring grasp of a new subject or situation, his innate fitness to command. General Buell was a professional soldier, he had the usual and natural contempt of a trained officer for an amateur commander, and yet, within a few hours after meeting Colonel Garfield, he gave him command of a brigade, and sent him to attack a superior enemy in his own way.

For his victory at Middle Creek Colonel

Garfield was made a Brigadier-General of Volunteers. He occupied, with his brigade, the valley of the Big Sandy River during the winter, and in the spring was ordered to report to General Buell, who, in command of the Army of the Ohio, was then near Nashville, Tennessee, hastening to unite with the army under General Grant at Shiloh, before the latter should be attacked by a superior Confederate army under General Johnston. On reaching the army under Buell, General Garfield was assigned to the command of the Twentieth Brigade, which he commanded with conspicuous ability during the second day's battle at Shiloh, where the timely arrival of General Buell's army enabled Grant to turn the tide of battle and win an important victory. General Garfield, still commanding his brigade, shared in the military operations before Corinth, and rebuilt the bridges and reopened the railway between Corinth and Decatur.

In November, 1862, he was ordered to Washington as a member of the Court-martial which tried General Fitz-John Porter for alleged misconduct in the field. General Hunter, who commanded a military department on the South Atlantic coast, was charmed with the qualities evinced by General Garfield during the trial, and applied to have him assigned to his command, but the application was refused, and Garfield was ordered to the Army of the Cumberland, which was then in camp at Murfreesboro', Tennessee, under command of General Rosecrans. It was customary in those days to designate the different independent armies of Federal troops operating against the Confederacy by the names of principal rivers in the region to which they were assigned. Thus, at the beginning of 1863, the period now under consideration, the Army of the Potomac was operating against Richmond; the Army of the Tennessee, under General Grant, was preparing

to invest Vicksburgh, in Mississippi; and the
Army of the Cumberland, to which had been
joined the Army of the Ohio since the battle
of Shiloh, was encamped, as already stated, at
Murfreesboro', thirty miles south-east of Nashville, the capital of Tennessee. The forces at
Murfreesboro' were at that time commanded by
General W. S. Rosecrans, and had recently
fought and won the sanguinary battle of Stone
River, one of the most stubbornly-contested en-
gagements of the war. The Confederate army
opposed to Rosecrans in this battle was commanded by General Bragg. The combatants
were nearly equally matched, and after two
days of heroic fighting, the wreck of the Confederate army retreated a few miles southward
into Alabama, and the forces under Rosecrans
had suffered such losses of men and equipment
as to require thorough reorganization before
they could again assume the offensive.

It was during this period of rest and reorganization that General Garfield, about the 20th of February, 1863, reached the head-quarters of General Rosecrans at Murfreesboro'. Colonel Garësche, Chief of Staff to Rosecrans, had been killed in the battle of Stone River, and his place had not yet been filled. "When Garfield arrived," says General Rosecrans in a recent letter, " I must confess I had a prejudice against him, as I understood he was a preacher who had gone into politics, and a man of that cast I was naturally opposed to. I found him to be a competent and efficient officer, an earnest and devoted patriot, and a man of the highest honour." Three days after his arrival General Garfield was assigned to duty as Chief of Staff of the Army of the Cumberland, and began the last and most important chapter of his military career. His first work was to organize a " Bureau of Military Information," similar in scope and purpose to that which has been developed to such remarkable efficiency in the

German army since 1866. This Bureau of Information was justly pronounced "the most
perfect machine of its kind organized during
the war."   By a system of reports obtained
through scouts, spies, Confederate prisoners,
loyal negroes, and captured official documents,
he prepared a comprehensive and accurate
exhibit of the strength and condition of Bragg's
army; the nature and quantity of his arms, ammunition, and supplies ; the sentiment prevailing
among his troops ; and the condition of the roads,
bridges, and railways throughout the enemy's
department. As the spring advanced, the
Government at Washington and popular opinion
began to demand that Rosecrans should advance.
But that officer, although in many respects an
admirable soldier, was absorbed with the details
of preparation, and had become involved in a
controversy with the Secretary of War. General
Garfield, who, in the course of two months, had
acquired an influence over his chief that was

almost absolute, laboured to promote a recon-
ciliation, and to prepare the army for an advance.
This aggressive policy was not supported by
the other officers, and the army lingered at
Murfreesboro' until June.   To every appeal
Rosecrans answered that he was not ready.
But Garfield, who knew, through his Bureau
of Information, the exact situation on both
sides, insisted that the time had come for a
decisive movement. . Finally, General Rosecrans submitted the matter in detail to
seventeen of his principal officers.   They
were commanders of corps, divisions, and
cavalry forces ; most of them were men of military education and large experience ; and each
was requested to state in writing his opinion of
the proper policy to be pursued and his reasons
for that opinion.   They all agreed with their
chief that the enemy was in superior force, in an
advantageous position, and that an attack by
the Union Army would be, under the circum-
stances, hazardous, and, in event of a repulse,

ruinous. General Garfield took the seventeen written opinions and prepared a reply which analyzed and answered every objection, and gave nine distinct and conclusive reasons why the army ought to immediately advance. This masterly paper showed that Rosecrans had 65,137 muskets and sabres to bring against 41,680 of the enemy. It concluded as follows : —" You have, in my judgment, wisely delayed a general movement hitherto, till your army could be massed and your cavalry could be mounted. Your mobile force can now be concentrated in twenty-four hours, and your cavalry, if not equal in numerical strength to that of the enemy, is greatly superior in efficiency. For these reasons I believe an immediate advance of all our available forces is advisable, and, under the providence of God, will be successful."

That report has been pronounced by an impartial historian,* "the ablest military document submitted by a Chief of Staff to his superior

* Mr. Whitelaw Reid.

during the war." Its logic was irresistible, and
the council of war before which it was read
decided that the army should move. Still, some
of the ablest officers distrusted the wisdom of
the movement, and one of them, General Crit-
tenden, who commanded an Army Corps, rode up
to General Garfield's tent on the morning of the
start, and said to him, " It is understood, sir, by
the general officers of the army, that this movement is your work. I wish you to understand
that it is a rash and fatal movement, for which
you will be held responsible." Then followed
the Tullahoma campaign, which Mr. Whitelaw
Reid in his admirable history describes as
" perfect in its conception, excellent in its general
execution, and only hindered from resulting in
the complete destruction of the opposing army
by the delays which had too long postponed its
movement."

This result naturally gave General Garfield
great *prestige* in the army, and he became more

than ever the indispensable lieutenant and adviser of his chief. It was a bitter thing for the major-generals who had been educated at West Point and spent their lives in the military service, to admit that in a great act of war the civilian brigadier from Hiram had a keener intelligence and a broader comprehension of grand tactics than they; but the success of the campaign silenced all controversy, and Garfield received the credit of his work.

Then began the advance on Chattanooga, an important railway centre on the Tennessee river, a hundred miles eastward from Tullahoma. Chattanooga was, in fact, the key to the whole central part of the Confederacy, and General Bragg, after his defeat in June, had retired thither with his army, assembled all available reinforcements, entrenched what was a naturally strong position, and prepared to make a desperate resistance. Chattanooga lies on the southern shore of the river, and in his advance

General Rosecrans boldly crossed to that side
and marched round far to the rear, hoping to
cut off Bragg's line of retreat and communica-
tions and crush his army against the river. The
Confederate General dared not risk being caught
in this trap, so he abandoned his position and
marched southward to secure a position from
which retreat, in case of defeat, would still be
possible. The mistake of one of Rosecrans'
corps commanders, who lost his way and had
to countermarch his column, delayed the advance of the Union army two days, and the
golden moment was lost. Instead of entrapping
Bragg's army at Chattanooga, Rosecrans encountered it in the densely wooded and rugged
valley of Chickamauga Creek, where, on the
19th of September, 1863, was fought another of
those bloody battles which left widows and
orphans in thousands of homes. There was
little opportunity for tactical movements, and the
two armies closed together at short range in the

thick woods and slew each other with relentless
valour. During the morning the fight had gone
rather in favour of the Union troops, when an
unforeseen and well-nigh fatal accident occurred.

General Garfield, as Chief of Staff to the commanding General, had written every General
Order issued during the battle, except one.
That one order, given during his momentary
absence, obscurely worded, misunderstood, and
literally obeyed by the officer to whom it was
addressed, caused a sudden and serious disaster.
The Army Corps commanded by General
McCook formed the right wing of Rosecrans'
line of battle. McCook's left division was
under command of General Wood, to whom
the unfortunate order was sent, directing him,
as he interpreted it, to withdraw his division
from the fighting line and move it to the rear of
the division on his left. Wood saw that the
manœuvre would be fatal, but it was ordered,
as he thought, and he felt constrained to execute

it. General Longstreet, who commanded the opposing Confederate line at that point, saw the blunder, hurled his powerful division into the gap left by Wood's withdrawal, and in twenty minutes the whole right wing of the Union army was broken, confused and falling back through the dense undergrowth towards Chattanooga. General Rosecrans with his Staff was borne back by the broken corps of McCook, and, believing the battle lost, started at a gallop for Chattanooga to rally his broken columns and prepare for defence. They had gone, perhaps, three miles, when the Chief of Staff pulled up his horse and told his General that the battle was not lost. He could hear the roar of heavy fighting where the Army of the Cumberland, led by General George H. Thomas, was holding the centre and left of the Federal line against the whole of Bragg's now confident legions. Garfield begged of Rose- crans permission to return to the front, find

General Thomas, and fight the battle out. It was his first taste of anything like defeat, and he could not endure the thought of leaving the field while a single regiment was capable of resistance. Attended only by a captain and two or three mounted orderlies, he set out on his perilous ride through the dense thickets and across ravines and hills. Often they encountered the enemy's skirmishers; an orderly was killed by Garfield's side, and his own horse wounded by a bullet, but he pushed on, and finally found the heroic Thomas, nearly surrounded, but yielding never an inch. As Garfield approached Thomas's position he saw Longstreet's corps massed in column, thrusting its front between the right of Thomas's line and the ridge of rising ground behind it. It was a perilous moment, but, warned and guided by Garfield, Thomas withdrew his right, formed a new line facing the advancing enemy, launched a fresh division, which had just reached the field, against Longstreet's advance, and the Army of the Cumberland was saved. The long, bloody day closed at last, and as the sun went down the Confederates, baffled and repulsed, withdrew from the fight. Garfield, on foot and enveloped in smoke, directed the pointing of a field battery, which, as the rebels retreated up the valley, flashed after them in the gathering darkness the last light that shone upon the red field of Chickamauga. Notwithstanding the disaster of the morning on the right, the battle was substantially a drawn one, and Rosecrans, retiring to Chattanooga, was secure from future attack.

This brilliant day's work, in which the Chief of Staff shared with General Thomas the first honours of that memorable engagement, practically ended General Garfield's military service. A few days after the battle he was sent by Rosecrans to Washington to report to the President and War Department in minute detail the situation and necessities of the army at Chattanooga. On arriving at the capital he found that he had been promoted to the rank of Major-General, " for gallant and meritorious services at the battle of Chickamauga ;" his commission dating from the 19th of September. He presented a full and satisfactory verbal report to the President and Secretary Stanton of the previous nine months' operations in Tennessee, and made so favourable an impression on President Lincoln that the latter advised him strongly to take what was, perhaps, the most unwilling, but which proved one of the most important, steps of his life.

The Republicans of the Nineteenth Congressional district of Ohio had, in October of the previous year, elected General Garfield to a seat in the Thirty-Eighth Congress, which was to assemble in December, 1863. It would be fourteen months from the date of his election before he would be required to take his place in Congress, and he had accepted the political promotion, fully expecting that the war would be over before the new Congress would assemble. But the war was yet unfinished, and General Garfield's situation, as December approached, became embarrassing. All his instincts prompted him to put aside the political honour and remain in the army. As a soldier he had not had many great opportunities, but he had made the utmost use of them all. He was one of the youngest major-generals in the service, he had won his rank fairly under fire, the country was applauding his conduct at Chickamauga, and the brightest laurels of the patriot soldier were just within his reach. Moreover, his gallant regiment, with battle-thinned ranks, and its colours riddled with the sharp hail of war, was still at the front, and he felt that it would be unworthy in him to leave the field while there was yet fighting to be done.

General Thomas offered him the command of a *corps d'armée* in the Army of the Cumberland, but President Lincoln was urgent in advising him to resign his commission and take his place in Congress. There was no want of brave and capable generals in the field, but there was, as the President strongly insisted, a crying need of men in Congress who understood the wants and requirements of the army, and were capable of dealing with the serious governmental · questions which were then pending.

The war had now been in progress more than two years. Vicksburgh, Gettysburgh, and other great battles had been won, but the Confederate armies were still in the field and the Confederacy was yet to be conquered. The war had settled down to one of endurance, a question of comparative resources and determination. It was clear that the Confederates would fight to the bitter end ; the problem was whether Congress, the Treasury, and the War Department, could marshal the superior numbers and resources of the North and throw their weight into the conflict. The first enthusiastic zeal which had filled the Union ranks with ardent volunteers had begun to cool as the long lists of dead and wounded were printed, and it was clear that the Congress of 1863–4 would have to deal with the difficult problem of conscription. The troops at the front had often been embarrassed by blunders and inexperience at Washington, and even the fellow-officers of General Garfield, much as they were attached to him, joined the President in urging him to resign and represent the army in Congress. Under these influences General Garfield gave up his commission, and took his seat as Representative on the 5th of December, 1863, a seat which he held in continuous service until his election as President in 1880, called him to a higher place. We must now follow him to the arena in which he has done the great permanent work of his life, and for which his previous experiences as a student, teacher, State Senator and soldier, were, so to speak, preparatory.

III.

GENERAL GARFIELD IN CONGRESS.

"IF you wish to know why an irredeemable paper currency is, and always has been, a curse to all the economic interests of this and all other countries, why confidence can be restored and maintained, why business can obtain a healthy development, why foreign commerce can be most profitably conducted only with a money system of staple and intrinsic value, you will find in the speeches of James A. Garfield upon this subject the most convincing information. You will find there opinions, not suddenly made up to order to suit an opportunity and the necessities of a candidate in an election, but the convictions of a lifetime carefully matured by conscientious research and large inquiry, and maintained with powerful reason, before they had become generally popular. You find there a teacher, statesman, and leader in a great movement, with principles so firmly grounded in his mind as well as his conscience that he would uphold them even were they not supported by a powerful party at his back."—Herr CARL SCHURZ.

THE State of Ohio is divided into twenty Congressional districts, designated by consecutive numbers. The Nineteenth District, which has been represented by General Garfield since

1863, is made up of four counties in the extreme north-eastern corner of the State. The district forms part of a tract of country lying along the southern shore of Lake Erie, and known as the "Western Reserve," from the fact that it was ceded in early days to the "Connecticut Land Company," and settled by a chosen community of pioneers from New England. The conditions of settlement offered especial advantages to officers and soldiers who had served creditably in the patriot armies during the War of the Revolution; and thither, in the early years of the present century, came the flower of the energetic, educated, conscientious people of the New England States. So distinctly have the descendants of these pioneers retained the characteristics of their ancestors, that the "Western Reserve" is to-day more like a portion of Massachusetts or Connecticut than any other similar district west of the Hudson River. It is a reading, thinking, praying community,

which is remarkably fastidious in its choice of
political representatives, keenly watchful of
their conduct, and loyal to them against all
opposition so long as they are faithful to their
trusts. Since the admission of Ohio to the
Union, the Nineteenth District had had but four
different representatives. For nearly a quarter
of a century Joshua R. Giddings, one of the
leading statesmen in American politics, had
stood for it. When, therefore, such a constituency placed the mantle of Mr. Giddings upon the
young Major-General, it was justly regarded
an extraordinary compliment. How well that
trust has been honoured and deserved only
those who are familiar with the work of
Congress during the past eighteen years can
adequately realize. In a sketch like this, the
writer is embarrassed by the impossibility of
giving in a limited space more than a faint out-
line of the great labours of General Garfield
during this period. His set speeches in impor-

tant debates would fill volumes. As was
justly said by Mr. Carl Schurz: " Scarcely a
single great measure of legislation was passed
during that long period without the imprint of
his mind. No man in Congress has devoted
such thorough inquiry to a large number of
important subjects, and formed upon them
opinions more matured and valuable."

Not only his speeches, but his labours upon
leading Committees, have been extraordinary.
Upon his entry into the House, he was naturally
assigned to the Committee of military affairs,
which was then grappling with the problems of
the war, at a time when a single serious mistake
in Congress might have imperilled the success
of the loyal cause. General Garfield was fresh
from the front of battle, he knew all the needs
of the army, and he became, almost from the
first, the controlling influence of the Committee.
From the chairmanship of the Military Committee he was promoted in 1869 to the head of

the Committee on Banking and Currency, which
was at that time charged with the important
duty of adjusting the national finances, after the
prolonged and serious strain which they had
undergone during the war period, to the conditions of peace.   At the same time he held a
leading place on the Committee of the Ninth
Census, which gave to the United States the
first comprehensive and well-digested census
that it had ever known. .

In 1872 General Garfield was again promoted
to the chairmanship of the Committee of
Appropriations, which is in many respects the
most important and influential committee of the
House.   Its business is to superintend and control, subject to the approval of Congress, all
expenditures made by the Government, for
whatever purpose. Separate Appropriation Bills
for the Army, the Navy, the Postal service, for
the Improvement of Rivers and Harbours, for the
Consular and Diplomatic service, in all eleven

distinct measures, in which each item of expenditure is estimated and recorded, are required to be prepared by the Committee of Appropriations at each annual session. The country was at that time clamouring for retrenchment in public expenditures and consequent reduction of taxation, so that the labour imposed upon General Garfield, during the four years in which he was head of the Appropriations Committee, was immense. So well was this work done by General Garfield and his immediate predecessors, that the expenses of the Government, which in 1865 had been $1,297,555,224, were reduced in 1875 to $287,133,874, which was conceded to be at that time the lowest practicable limit of judicious economy.

The country was during 1874–5 in the depth of the financial depression and distress which followed the collapse and panic of 1873. The paper currency, which had floated the Treasury through the war, had served the purpose for which it had been created, but had inevitably inaugurated a period of inflated and fictitious values. Disregarding the solemn and eloquent warnings of General Garfield and some of his more discerning colleagues, Congress had refused, immediately after the return of peace, to contract the inflated currency and bring the business of the country back to a basis of real values. It was on the 16th of March, 1866, less than a year after the surrender of the Confederate armies, that General Garfield had first declared his views on the subject of the currency, in a speech which reached down to the fundamental principles of wise and honest finance. The Bill under consideration was a measure conferring upon the Secretary of the Treasury the same powers in funding the debt which Secretary Sherman recently employed with such admirable effect, and providing for a gradual but early return to specie pay-ments. General Garfield's speech in support of the measure was a masterpiece. His closing sentences were prophetic :

"We leave it to the House to decide which alternative it will choose. Choose the one, and you float away into an unknown sea of paper money that shall know no decrease until you take just such a measure as is now proposed to bring us back to solid values. Delay the measure, and it will cost the country dear. Adopt it now, and with a little depression in business, and a little stringency in the money market, the worst will be over, and we shall have reached the solid earth. Sooner or later such a measure must be adopted. Go on as you are now going on, and a financial crisis worse than that of 1837 will bring us to the bottom. · I for one am not willing that my name shall be linked to the fate of a paper currency. I believe that any party which commits itself to paper money will go down amid the general disaster, covered with the curses of a ruined people."

" Mr. Speaker, I remember that on the monument of Queen Elizabeth, where her glories were recited and her honours summed up, among .the last and the highest, recorded as the climax of her honours, was this—that she had restored the money of her kingdom to its just value. And when this House shall have done its work, when it shall have brought back values to their proper standard, it will deserve a monument."

But Congress lacked the courage to follow such sound advice. The country was in the first ecstasies of intoxicating speculation and expansion. Business was everywhere flourishing, and fortunes were being rapidly accumulated— in depreciated paper. The orgie of speculation reached its climax in 1872, and in September of the year following the bubble burst. When Congress was organized in 1874, the best ability in the House was needed on the Committee of Ways and Means. Expenditures had been reduced to their lowest practical limit, but business

was prostrate ; all values were broken and un-
settled, and the problem of the hour was to
adjust the essential taxation to the depressed
condition of trade and the straitened resources
of the people. Instinctively public opinion
turned to Garfield, and he was appointed Chairman of Ways and Means. A record of his
services in that position might fill a volume and
furnish ample and conclusive reasons why, in
the great party crisis at Chicago last June, the
people again turned to him as the man best
capable of leading them through a difficult situation to an important triumph. Enough has
perhaps been said of General Garfield's service
in committees to serve the purposes of this
sketch and show the rank that he attained as a
financier during a period which demanded and
developed the highest powers of economic state-
craft. It remains now within the limits of this
chapter to give from the great mass of his
speeches a few brief extracts which may serve

to illustrate his position upon leading questions of legislation.

FINANCE.

In respect to the finances, he maintained, throughout the long struggle which ended with the resumption of specie payments in 1879, the same clear consistent attitude that was foreshadowed in his speech of March 16th, 1866, from which a passage has already been quoted. For years he had been an exhaustive and discriminating student of English finance. The whole record of British legislation on commerce and currency during the past two centuries had been studied, until every important fact was at his ready command. In May, 1868, when the country was rapidly drifting into a hopeless confusion of ideas on financial subjects, and when several prominent statesmen had come forward with specious plans for creating " absolute money," by putting the Government stamp upon bank notes, and for paying off with

this false currency the bonds which the nation
had solemnly agreed to pay in gold, General
Garfield stood up, almost single-handed, and
faced the current with a speech which any
statesman of this century might be proud to
have written on his monument. · It embraced
twenty-three distinct but concurrent topics, and
occupied in delivery an entire day's session of
the House.   After recognizing candidly all the
discouraging facts of the situation, and admitting
that the United States had less experience with
such vast problems than any other civilized
nation, he went on to say :—" The dollar is the
gauge that measures every blow of the axe,
every swing of the scythe, every stroke of the
hammer,. every faggot that blazes on the poor
man's hearth, every fabric that clothes his
children, every mouthful that feeds their hunger.
The word dollar is a substantive word, the
fundamental condition of every contract, of
every sale, of every payment, whether from the

national treasury or from the stand of the apple-woman in the street.   Now, what is our situation ?   There has been no day since the 25th of February, 1862, when any man could tell what would be the value of our legal currency dollar the next month or the next day.   Since that day we have substituted for a dollar the printed promise of the Government to pay a dollar.   That promise we have broken.   We have suspended payment ; and have, by law, compelled the citizen to receive dishonoured · paper instead of money."

And in conclusion :—" For my own part, my course is taken.   In view of all the facts of our situation, of all the terrible experiences of the past, both at home and abroad, and of the united testimony of the wisest and bravest statesmen who have lived and laboured during the past century, it is my firm conviction that any considerable increase of the volume of our inconvertible paper money will shatter public credit, will paralyze public industry, and oppress the poor; and that the gradual restoration of our ancient standard of value will lead us, by the safest and surest paths, to national prosperity and the steady pursuits of peace."

The measure which he opposed was defeated, but in the following July the hydra-headed fallacy reappeared in the form of a Bill authorizing the taxation of United States bonds. Garfield was again the man in the breach, with a prompt and powerful protest, which concluded with these words :—

"Mr. Speaker, I desire to say, in conclusion, that in my opinion all these efforts to pursue a doubtful and unusual, if not dishonourable policy in reference to our public debt, spring from a lack of faith in the intelligence and conscience of the American people. Hardly an hour passes when we do not hear it whispered that some such policy as this must be adopted, or the people will by-and-by repudiate the debt.

For my own part, I do not share that distrust. The people of this country have shown, by the highest proofs Nature can give, that wherever the path of duty and honour may lead, however steep and rugged it may be, they are ready to walk it. They feel the burden of the public debt, but they remember that it is the price of blood—the precious blood of half a million brave men who died to save to us all that makes life desirable or property secure. I believe they will, after a full hearing, discard all methods of paying their debts by sleight-of-hand, or by any scheme which crooked wisdom may devise. If public morality did not protest against any such plan, enlightened public selfishness would refuse its sanction. Let us be true to our trust a few years longer, and the next generation will be here with its seventy-five millions of population and its sixty billions of wealth. To them the debt that then remains will be a light burden. They will pay the last bond according to the

letter and spirit of the contract, with the same
sense of grateful duty with which they will pay ·
the pensions of the few surviving soldiers of the ·
great war for the Union."

The Secretary of the Treasury at that time,
fearing that the heresies uttered by the inflationists would seriously compromise the national credit
abroad, had the two speeches of General Garfield
published in pamphlet form and sent to leading
financiers and statesmen in Europe.   A copy of
the pamphlet happened to fall into the hands of
Mr. John Bright, who showed it to Mr. Glad-
stone.   Upon their motion, General Garfield
was elected an honorary member of the Reform
Club, a compliment which was, under the cir-
cumstances, peculiarly gratifying.

These brief extracts from speeches delivered
by General Garfield at a time when Congress
and an overwhelming majority of the people,
particularly in the Western States, were opposed
to him, will sufficiently illustrate the soundness

of his financial principles, and the unflinching courage with which he stood by his guns during the entire discussion. In reference to

THE TARIFF

his record is equally positive and clear. At Williams' College he was as a student schooled in political economy by Professor Perry, who was then, as now, one of the leading American advocates of Free Trade. The text-book was Wayland's "Political Economy," but young Garfield was not a student who followed blindly any teacher or text-book. He read all collateral authorities which the college library could supply, and did his own thinking. At the close of the term, Professor Perry asked him what had been his conclusions in respect to Protection, and the reply was so definite and characteristic that the instructor wrote it down in his memorandum-book. "As an abstract theory," said Garfield, "the doctrine of Free Trade seems to be

universally true ; but as a question of practica-
bility, *in a country like ours,* the protective
system seems to be indispensable."

It has cost General Garfield no little annoy-
ing criticism to be perfectly loyal, as he has
always been, to this exact line of his convictions
respecting the tariff.   His constituents in Ohio
are heavily engaged in mining and various
forms of the iron manufacture; and naturally
have been clamorous for high duties.   The
Republicans, as a party, have advocated a protective tariff, and about once in two years since
General Garfield entered Congress a new Tariff
Bill has been incubated and discussed.   He
has always taken a leading part in these dis-
cussions, and always with characteristic clear-
ness and consistency.   His creed was declared
in 1866 in these words :—

"We have seen that one extreme school of
economists would place the price of all manu-
factured articles in the hands of foreign pro-

ducers by rendering it impossible for our manufacturers to compete with them ; while the other
extreme school, by making it impossible for the
foreigner to sell his competing wares in our
market, would give the people no immediate
check upon the prices which our manufacturers
might fix for their products. I disagree with
both these extremes. I hold that a properly
adjusted competition between home and foreign
products is the best gauge by which to regulate
international trade. Duties should be so high
that our manufacturers can fairly compete with
the foreign product, but not so high as to
enable them to drive out the foreign article,
enjoy a monopoly of the trade, and regulate the
price as they please. This is my doctrine of
Protection. If Congress pursues this line of
policy steadily, we shall year by year approach
more nearly to the basis of Free Trade, because
we shall be more nearly able to compete with
other nations on equal terms. *I am for a*

Protection which leads to ultimate Free Trade.
I am for that Free Trade which can only be
achieved through a reasonable Protection."

The subject recurred in a protracted and determined debate during the Session of 1878, when
General Garfield, developing the argument
which he had outlined first in 1866, said:—
" The men who created this Constitution also
set it in operation, and developed their own
idea of its character.   That idea was unlike any
other that then prevailed upon the earth.   They
made the general welfare of the people the great
source and foundation of the common.defence.
In all the nations of the Old World the public
defence was provided for by the great standing
armies, navies, and fortified posts, so that the
nation might every moment be fully armed
against danger from without or turbulence within.
Our fathers said : ' Though we will use the
taxing power to maintain a small army and navy
sufficient to keep alive the knowledge of war,

yet the main reliance for our defence shall be
the intelligence, culture, and skill of our people ;
a development of our own intellectual and
material resources, which will enable us to
do everything that may be necessary to equip,
clothe, and feed ourselves in time of war, and
make ourselves intelligent, happy, and prosperous in peace."

*   *   *   *   *

" Too much of our Tariff discussion has been
warped by narrow and sectional considerations.
But when we base our action upon the conceded
national importance of the great industries I
have referred to, when we recognize the fact
that artisans and their products are essential to
the well-being of our country, it follows that
there is no dweller in the humblest cottage on
our remotest frontier who has not a deep
personal interest in the legislation that shall
promote these great national industries. Those
arts that enable our nation to rise in the scale of

civilization bring their blessings to all, and patriotic citizens will cheerfully bear a fair share of the burden necessary to make their country great and self-sustaining. I will defend a tariff that is national in its aims, that protects and sustains those interests without which the nation cannot become great and self-sustaining."

Then, coming back to the impregnable doctrine that national safety and independence under a Republican Government are dependent upon national development, he concluded : "So important, in my view, is the ability of the nation to manufacture all these articles necessary to arm, equip, and clothe our people, that if it could not be secured in any other way I would vote to pay money out of the Federal Treasury to maintain Government iron and steel, woollen and cotton mills, at whatever cost. Were we to neglect these great interests and depend upon other nations, in what a condition of helplessness would we find ourselves when we should be again involved in war with the very nations on whom we were depending to furnish us these supplies ?   The system adopted by our fathers is wiser, for it so encourages the great national industries as to make it possible at all times for our people to equip themselves for war, and at the same time increase their intelligence and skill so as to make them better fitted for all the duties of citizenship both in war and in peace. *We provide for the common defence by a system which promotes the general welfare.*"

SILVER MONEY.

There was one other form of financial folly against which Mr. Garfield made a gallant though ineffectual resistance.   During the existence of the Forty-fifth Congress, from December, 1877, until March, 1879, there sprang up a movement in favour of the unlimited coinage of silver. The lower branch of Congress was controlled by a democratic majority which had revolted

against the established law providing for the resumption of specie payments on January 1st,
1879. A Bill had been passed repealing the
Resumption Law, but it had been promptly
vetoed by President Hayes, and the anti-re--
sumption party could not muster the requisite
two-thirds majority in both branches of Congress
to pass the Bill over the Presidential veto.
Failing in this, the reactionists sought to gratify
a supposed public demand for a "cheap currency"
by flooding the country with a silver coinage of
deficient weight and value. The scheme was
an act of demagogism, appealing to popular
duplicity and ignorance.

The silver fallacy was strongly supported by
the wealthy and influential association of men who
owned rich and productive mines on the Pacific
Coast, and who feared that by reason of the
demonetization of silver that was then going on
in Europe, the metal would become redundant
and depreciated in value. A Mr. Bland, of

Missouri, introduced into the House a Bill to establish a standard silver dollar, having a weight of $412\frac{1}{2}$ grains, and to restore the legal tender character of silver coin which had been abolished several years before. The Bill also authorized the unlimited coinage of these short-weight dollars at Government expense.

General Garfield opposed the measure with all his ability, not because he was opposed to the use of silver as money, but because $412\frac{1}{2}$ grains of silver were not worth a dollar, nor likely, in the existing state of things, to ever become so, and because he did not think it wise at that time for the United States to undertake single-handed and alone to rehabilitate silver as a legal tender coinage and establish an arbitrary ratio of value between that metal and gold. His speeches during the debate were fearless and masterly, and drew upon him the sharp criticism of some of his colleagues, who have long since acknowledged that he was right and they were wrong. On the 17th of May, he made a leading speech against the Bill of Mr. Bland, the tenor of which may be inferred from the following passage: "And yet," said he, "outside of this Capitol, I do not this day know of a single great and recognized advocate of bimetallic money who regards it prudent or safe for any nation largely to increase the coinage standard of silver coin at the present time beyond the limits fixed by existing laws. France and the States of the Latin Union, that have long believed in bimetallism, maintained it against all comers, and have done all in their power to advocate it throughout the world, dare not coin a single silver coin, and have not done so since 1874. The most strenuous advocates of bimetallism in those countries say it would be ruinous to bimetallism for France or the Latin Union to coin any more silver at present. The remaining stock of German silver now for sale, amounting to from forty to seventy-five millions of dollars, is a standing menace to the exchange and silver coinage of Europe. One month ago the leading financial journal of London proposed that the Bank of England buy one half of the German surplus and hold it five years on condition that the German Government shall hold the other half off the market. The time is ripe for some wise and prudent arrangement among the nations to save silver from a disastrous break-down." . . . . " Yet we, who during the past two years have coined far more silver dollars than we ever before coined since the foundation of the Government —ten times as many as we coined during half a century of our national life—are to-day ignoring and defying the enlightened, universal opinion of bimetallists, and saying that the United States, single-handed and alone, can enter the field and settle the mighty issue alone. We are justifying the old proverb that ' Fools rush in where angels fear to tread.' "

Subsequent events justfied his predictions.

The House passed the Bland Bill, which then went to the Senate for concurrence. The Senate passed it with an amendment limiting the coinage of silver to four million dollars per month. The House concurred in the Senate's amendment, and the President vetoed the Bill. Both branches of Congress then passed the Act over the executive veto, and it became a law. The result is that the vaults of the United States Treasury are to-day gorged with silver dollars, each of which contains about 89 cents worth of silver and eleven cents worth of Congressional alloy. The people will not have them or use them in any quantity, and the Mints of the Government, which are needed for the coinage of gold, are compelled under the law, to go on coining the redundant and useless silver dollars which are at this time the only serious disturbing element in American finance.

Among the other invaluable services of General Garfield during his career in Congress have been his fearless and patriotic expositions of Constitutional principles in crises of intense partisan excitement. A notable example of this occurred during the special Session of 1879. The second and final Session of the Forty-fifth Congress expired on the 4th of March of that year. During the winter the democratic majority which controlled the House had attempted to pass three Acts of independent political legislation by attaching them to the Appropriation Bills which provided money for the support of the Government. These obnoxious measures were, 1, "The repeal of the jurors' test oath; 2, a material modification of the existing law defining the functions of the army; and 3, an Act repealing certain laws which govern the election of members of Congress." In the quarrel which ensued, the limit of the Session was passed, and the President was compelled to convene the forty-sixth or new Congress immediately after the 4th of March, in order that the necessary appropriations might be made before the 30th of June, the close of the fiscal year. The same Bills were again presented, and the democratic leaders announced their purpose to compel the President to approve them, including the amendment curtailing the constitutional functions of the Federal Marshals, or, in default of that approval, to destroy the power of the Government, by withholding its supplies. (To make the situation clear, it should be remembered that no American President or Cabinet officer can use any money of the Treasury for any purpose until it has been expressly appropriated for that purpose by Congress.)

This attempt to coerce the Executive was first challenged and exposed by General Garfield on the 29th of March, in a speech which thrilled the country, and made its author not only the head and front of his own party, but the advocate of all men of either party who held Constitutional government above partisan advantage. Two paragraphs from the speech will show the drift of its argument :

" Mr. CHAIRMAN : I have no hope of being able to convey to the members of this House my own conviction of the very great gravity and solemnity of the crisis which this decision of the Chairman of the Committee of the Whole has brought upon this country. I wish I could be proved a false prophet in reference to the result of this action. I wish I could be over-whelmed with the proof that I am utterly mis-taken in my views. But no view I have ever taken has entered more deeply and more seriously into my convictions than this : that this House has to-day resolved to enter upon a revolution against the Constitution and Govern-ment of the United States. I do not know that that intention exists in the minds of half the representatives who occupy the other side of this hall. I hope it does not. I am ready to

believe it does not exist to any large extent.
But I mean to say the consequence of the programme just adopted, if persisted in, is nothing
less than the total subversion of this Government."

*   *   *   *   *

"Our theory of law is free consent. That is
the granite foundation of our whole superstruc-
ture. Nothing in the Republic can be law
without consent—the free consent of the House;
the free consent of the Senate; the free consent
of the Executive, or, if he refuse it, the free
consent of two-thirds of these bodies. Will any
man deny that? Will any man challenge a word
of the statement that free consent is the foundation rock of all our institutions? And yet the
programme announced two weeks ago was, that
if the Senate refused to consent to the demand
of the House, the Government should stop.
And the proposition was then, and the programme is now, that, although there is not a

Senate to be coerced, there is still a third independent branch in the legislative power of the Government, whose consent is to be coerced at the peril of the destruction of this Government ; that is, if the President, in the discharge of his duty, shall exercise his plain constitutional right to refuse his consent to this proposed legislation, the Congress will so use its voluntary powers as to destroy the Government. This is the proposition which we confront; and we denounce it as revolution."

" The proposition now is, that after fourteen years have passed and not one petition from one American citizen has come to us asking that this law be repealed, while not one memorial has found its way to our desks complaining of the law, so far as I have heard, the Democratic House of Representatives now hold that if they are not permitted to force upon another House and upon the Executive, against their consent, the repeal of a law that Democrats made, this

refusal shall be considered a sufficient ground
for starving this Government to death."

SPEECHES OF OCCASION.

But the oratorical services of General Garfield during the years of his maturity have not
been limited to his work in Congress. On
many important occasions he has been the
chosen orator, and has uniformly acquitted himself with consummate credit. On the border of
Virginia, across the Potomac river from the City
of Washington, there stands on the crest of
Arlington Heights a stately mansion which was
formerly the home of General Robert E. Lee,
the Commander-in-Chief of the Confederate
Armies. During the war the estate was used
as a burial-ground for thousands of Union
soldiers killed in the battles in Virginia, or who
had died of wounds or disease in the hospitals
at Washington. The ancestral farm became
one vast burial-ground, and after the war it was

appropriated by the Government, handsomely laid out with walks and drives, and solemnly dedicated as a sacred and permanent resting-place of the dead. The dedication took place on the 30th of May, 1868, the anniversary designated by law as a memorial day on which the graves of Union soldiers throughout the United States are wreathed and strewn with flowers by a grateful people. At the dedication of Arlington Cemetery, General Garfield spoke in presence of a vast audience, including the President, the Cabinet, leading members of the Diplomatic Corps, and eminent citizens from all parts of the country. He said :

" If silence is ever golden, it must be here, beside the graves of fifteen thousand men whose lives were more significant than speech, and whose death was a poem, the music of which can never be sung. With words, we plight faith, make promises, praise virtues. Promises may not be kept ; plighted faith may be only the cunning mask of vice. We do not know one promise these men made, one pledge they gave, one word they spoke; but we do know they summed up and perfected, by one supreme act, the highest virtues of men and citizens. For love of country they accepted death; and thus resolved all doubts, and made immortal their patriotism and their virtue.

"For the noblest man that lives there still remains a conflict. He must still withstand the assaults of time and fortune; must still be assailed with temptations before which lofty natures have fallen. But with *these*, the conflict ended; the victory was won when death stamped on them the great seal of heroic character, and closed a record which years can never blot."

*   *   *   *   *

"The view from this spot bears some resemblance to that which greets the eye at Rome. In sight of the Capitoline Hill, up and across the Tiber, and overlooking the city, is a hill, not rugged or lofty, but known as the Vatican Mount. At the beginning of the Christian era an imperial circus stood on its summit. There, gladiator slaves died for the sport of Rome, and wild beasts fought with wilder men. In that arena a Galilean fisherman gave up his life a sacrifice for his faith. No human life was ever so nobly avenged. On that spot was reared the proudest Christian temple ever built by human hands. For its adornment the rich offerings of every clime and kingdom had been contributed. And now, after eighteen centuries, the hearts of two hundred million people turn toward it with reverence when they worship God. As the traveller descends the Apennines, he sees the dome of St. Peter rising above the desolate Campagna and the dead city, long before the Seven Hills and ruined palaces appear to his view. The fame of the dead fisherman has outlived the glory of the Eternal City. A noble life, crowned with heroic deeds, rises above and outlives the pride and pomp and glory of the mightiest empire of the earth."

There was another occasion which called out General Garfield's powers as an obituary speaker, and illustrated the strong feeling of comradeship between himself and his colleagues with which no merely partisan considerations have ever been permitted to interfere. Among the Democratic members of the House in 1878–9 was the Hon. Gustave Schleicher from Texas. Mr. Schleicher was a German who had emigrated to Texas many years ago, and had become one of the most influential men in that State. He was a man of finished education, strong and enlightened principles, and there had grown up between him and General Garfield a mutual affection like that of brothers. In February, 1879, Mr. Schleicher died, and, in accordance with custom, the House passed resolutions of respect to his memory. Pending the adoption of the resolutions, General Garfield delivered an eulogy, from which the following is an extract :—

" I stand with reverence in the presence of such a life and such a career as that of Gustave Schleicher. It illustrates more strikingly than almost any life I know the mystery that envelops that product which we call character, and which is the result of two great forces: the initial force which the Creator gave it when He called the man into being; and the force of all the external influence and culture that mould and modify the development of a life.

" In contemplating the first of these elements, no power of analysis can exhibit all the latent forces enfolded in the spirit of a new-born child, which derive their origin from the thoughts and deeds of remote ancestors, and, enveloped in the awful mystery of life, have been trans-mitted from generation to generation across forgotten centuries. Each new life is thus 'the heir of all the ages.'

" Applying these reflections to the character of

Gustave Schleicher, it may be justly said that we have known few men in whose lives were concentrated so many of the deeply interesting elements that made him what he was. We are accustomed to say, and we have heard to-night, that he was born on foreign soil. In one sense that is true; and yet in a very proper historic sense he was born in our fatherland. One of the ablest of recent historians begins his opening volume with the declaration that England is not the fatherland of the English-speaking people, but the ancient home, the real fatherland of our race, is the ancient forests of Germany. The same thought was suggested by Montesquieu long ago, when he declared in his 'Spirit of Law' that the British Constitution came out of the woods of Germany.

"To this day the Teutonic races maintain the same noble traits that Tacitus describes in his admirable history of the manners and character of the Germans. We may therefore say that the friend whose memory we honour to-night is one of the elder brethren of our race.   He came to America direct from our fatherland, and not, like our own fathers, by the way of England.

*   *   *   *   *

" His career as a member of this House has exhibited the best results of all these influences of nature and nurture.   He has done justice· to the scholarship which Germany gave him and the large and comprehensive ideas with which life in the New World inspired him."

AS A CONSTITUTIONAL LAWYER.

General Garfield began the study of law during the years of his service as teacher and President of Hiram College.   He carried his law books to the field during the war, and studied during his hours of leisure when his comrades were asleep.   He continued his studies in Washington with such success that in

1868 he was retained in a case of national importance before the Supreme Court. In 1864, several men had been tried by a Military Commission in the State of Indiana for treason in preventing enlistments and encouraging desertions from the army. They were condemned and sentenced to death. President Lincoln commuted their sentence to imprisonment for life, and after the war their case was revived and brought before the Supreme Court of the United States on the plea that a Military Commission had no proper jurisdiction, even during a time of war, in a State or district where the Civil Courts were undisturbed and in full exercise of their powers. The case was one which clearly involved a fundamental principle of Constitutional Government, and as the culprits had been guilty of a heinous crime at a time when such treachery as theirs might have imperilled the Union cause, it required great courage on the part of a young Republican Congressman to come

before the Court of Last Appeal and make an
argument which, if successful, would set them at
liberty. General Garfield's associate counsel
were all Democrats, the very head and front of
the legal profession in America. Nevertheless,
he saw the vital principle involved, went before
the Court, and made the first speech, which
covered the whole ground and contributed
powerfully towards influencing the final decision
in favour of his clients. After reviewing the
most noteworthy precedents in English law,
he said : " They enable us to trace from its far-
off source the progress and development of
Anglo-Saxon liberty ; its innumerable conflicts
with irresponsible power ; its victories, dearly
bought, but always won—victories which have
crowned with immortal honours the institutions
of England, and left their indelible impress upon
the Anglo-Saxon mind. These principles our
fathers brought with them to the New World,
and guarded with sleepless vigilance and religious

devotion. In its last hour of trial, during the last rebellion, the Republic did not forget them.

* * * * *

"The only ground upon which the learned counsel attempt to establish the authority of the Military Commission to try the petitioners is that of the necessity of the case. I answer, there was no such necessity. Neither the Constitution nor Congress recognized it. I point to the Constitution as an arsenal stored with ample powers to meet every emergency of national life. No higher test of its completeness can be imagined than has been afforded by the great rebellion, which dissolved the Municipal Governments of Eleven States, and consolidated them into a gigantic traitorous government *de facto*, inspired with the desperate purpose of destroying the Government of the United States. From the beginning of the rebellion to its close, Congress by its legislation kept pace with the necessities of the nation. In sixteen carefully considered laws, the National Legislature undertook to provide for every contingency, and arm the Executive at every point with the solemn sanction of law."

Finally, to the court :

" Your decision will mark an era in American history. The just and final settlement of this great question will take a high place among the great achievements which have immortalized this decade. It will establish for ever this truth, of inestimable value to us and to mankind, that a republic can wield the vast enginery of war without breaking down the safeguards of liberty; can suppress insurrection and put down rebellion, however formidable, without destroying the bulwarks of law; can, by the might of its armed milllons, preserve and defend both nationality and liberty. Victories on the field were of priceless value, for they plucked the life of the Republic out of the hands of its enemies : but

> " Peace hath her victories
> No less renowned than war ;"

and if the protection of law shall, by your decision, be extended over every acre of our peaceful territory, you will have rendered the great decision of the century."

With these disjointed and meagre quotations from General Garfield's published speeches we take leave of this portion of his record. We omit, as of a partisan character, all extended reference to his shining renown as a speaker from the hustings in political campaigns. In this field of service he has no superior, and but few rivals, among the leaders of either political party in America. He is a bulwark of strength to the Republican cause in every closely contested election, and his aid is always invoked in critical contests. When, in the autumn of 1878, the paper money inflationists in Massachusetts, under the leadership of Benjamin F. Butler, threatened to gain control of that State, General Garfield was the man chosen by common consent to go to the rescue. Before an immense and turbulent audience at Fanueil Hall he made a most convincing speech, answered with telling effect the questions of the mob, and contributed greatly toward the victory of sound principles which followed the canvass.

HOW AND WHY HE WAS NOMINATED FOR PRESIDENT.

It must be apparent from what has preceded that the choice of a recognized party leader like General Garfield as a nominee for President was, after all, a natural and creditable result. The National Convention at Chicago included 756 delegates, of whom General Garfield was one. Its sessions were held in a vast building capable of seating fifteen thousand persons. Every inch of available space outside the area and rostrum reserved for the delegates, was crowded, during the prolonged sessions of the Convention, with an eager and attentive audience, in which the best culture and influence of the country were represented. Ex-President Grant was supported for the nomination by a strong constituency, led by Senator Conkling, of New York; Senator Blaine, from Maine, was advocated by a numerous and devoted body of followers. A third division, led by General Garfield, advocated the nomination of Mr. Sherman, whose able administration of the Treasury during the trying period of resumption had given him great popularity among the financial and business classes. But neither of these three aspirants could command a majority of the delegates. For several days, during some of which the sessions were prolonged far into the evening, the battle hung in even scale. The proceedings of each day were telegraphed over the country and read the next morning with intense interest by millions of people. General Garfield's speech in presenting Mr. Sherman's name as a candidate had made a profound impression in the Convention and throughout the country. Repeatedly, when the situation became dangerously exciting, he mounted the platform, and by his calm practical advice and strict justice between opposing elements, soothed the disputants and restored harmony. The Convention recognized in him a dominating personal influence, a leader whom no selfish motive could swerve from absolute fair dealing between the rival interests. However great the excitement that prevailed, when General Garfield rose in his seat or appeared on the platform to speak the vast audience became suddenly silent. There could be no more direct proof of popular leadership than this—that he was almost the only man whom that great Convention would always listen to with attention. And so, when the evenly balanced strength of the other candidates and the asperities between their supporters produced a dead-lock, which kept the country in suspense from day to day, the people recognized who had become the real master of the Convention, and sent letters and telegrams with the terse suggestion "Take Garfield." The Convention obeyed : the nomination was made, all conflicting factions and interests were harmonized, and a triumphant election at the polls in November was the natural result.

It may be naturally asked why General Garfield, possessing all these desirable qualities, was not early put forward as an aspirant for the nomination, like Grant and Sherman and Blaine. There were obvious and sufficient reasons for this. In the first place General Garfield is no " manager." He has never asked for an office nor permitted his friends to do so for him. For eighteen years, as we have seen, he had been elected as the representative of the most exacting and critical constituency in the country. He had

served long and faithfully, and he looked forward
longingly to a period of comparative rest in the
scholarly, dignified atmosphere of the Senate. A
seat in the Senate had been easily within his
reach during the spring of 1877, but President
Hayes had just taken the Executive Chair with
a majority in the House opposed to him, and he
besought General Garfield to remain in that body,
to lead the Republican minority and develop
its utmost strength in support of the Administration. With characteristic unselfishness
General Garfield had complied with this request,
and two years later the Legislature of Ohio had,
by a unanimous vote of all its Republican
members, elected him to the seat in the United
States Senate then occupied by Senator Thur-
man. With this rate of progress General Garfield and his friends were fully satisfied. To
have been chosen Senator by a unanimous vote
in a hotly contested political State like Ohio, was
an unprecedented compliment. Few of his

friends doubted that if he should live he would become President; but he was still young, his place in the Senate had been won, and for higher honours he could well trust to the future.

There is another fact which bears directly upon this point. A majority of the American people, and General Garfield among them, have come to regard the Presidency of the Republic as too great a distinction to be aspired to and won by the ordinary methods of political management. They prefer to retain that supreme honour as a gift to be bestowed rather than a prize to be sought. The unplanned and spontaneous nomination of Abraham Lincoln in 1860 was the precedent which, more than any other, turned the instinct of popular selection towards General Garfield in 1880. Not because they aspired to the Presidency, but because they were deemed worthy of it these two men were called by the people to that exalted station of power and responsibility.

IV.

PERSONALLY.

Physically, as well as mentally, General Garfield represents the full stature of manhood. He is more than six feet in height, with broad shoulders, a massive head, and a robust muscular frame. He began life with a sound constitution, which was well developed by his outdoor labour during the growing years of boyhood. This advantage he has retained by a temperate, well-ordered life, in which the only form of dissipation has been overwork—the long vigils which he has held over his books when most other men were seeking enjoyment or asleep. Reading is with him a passion which absorbs most of the leisure which can be gleaned from his busy life. In times of greatest preoccupation he goes to books for recreation and rest. The writer

remembers once, near the close of a Congressional Session, when General Garfield was
burthened with the responsibilities of the Chairmanship of Appropriations, finding him alone in
his library, long after midnight, full of delight over
something new that he had found in a Greek
history or poem about Pericles and Aspasia.
He had been reading systematically, he said, for
a week or two past, about the renowned lovers
in history, and had been enchanted. Abelard
and Héloise, Pericles and Aspasia, Dante and
Beatrice, Chopin and Georges Sand, and a dozen
other historical couples, had been before his
literary telescope during the leisure moments of
the previous fortnight, and he was so full of the
subject that for the time he could talk of
nothing else. That incident illustrates his
method of reading. He reads systematically,
exhausts a subject and files the results away in
his unerring memory for future use or enjoyment. He reads most of the really good novels

as they appear, and has certain standard favour-
ites, like " Pickwick" and " Pendennis," to which
he returns for refreshment as people go to the
mountains in summer for fresh air.   Often as
he has read the first chapters of " Pickwick" he
has never finished it, because, as he says, its
author being dead, such another book cannot
be written, and he wants to keep some part of
it fresh and untouched for the future. His love
for classic poetry is supreme among his literary
tastes.   During all his service in the army he
carried a volume of Horace in his pocket, and
among his recently published correspondence
are found long letters written to a class-mate
from the scene of great military events, dis-
cussing nice shades of construction in certain
passages of his favourite poet.   He learned the
German language for the love of it and in
order to reach the treasures of its literature;
and he mastered the French tongue while in
Congress so that he might more thoroughly

study the financial history of France during the political mutations which have disturbed that country. He is also a tireless student of the English language, and finds the keenest enjoyment in etymological research. He tracks a complex word back through all its derivations to the original root with the ardour of a sportsman in the pursuit of game.

His nature is sympathetic and naturally confiding. His weakest point as a politician is that he sees some of his own sincerity reflected in other men and believes them better and truer than they sometimes are. His ardent love of letters does not make him in any sense bookish or pedantic; he is, on the contrary, eminently a social and companionable person, and enjoys calling intimate friends by their first names.

He has two homes—one, a plain comfortable brick dwelling, which he built some years ago in Washington, the other a neat country-house of

Gothic architecture on his farm a few miles east of Cleveland. To that farm he goes with his family in May or June, after the close of the Congressional Session, and gives himself up to the relaxation of farming; no dainty, lily-handed pretence, but actual labour in the field with his men. Politicians and Congressional associates who go to "Woodlawn" during the summer months to talk over affairs of State, generally make a journey over the farm and learn something about his cattle and crops before the day is over.

He is not a "society man" in the conventional sense, but he delights in the society of refined and intellectual women. The meetings of the Washington Literary Association, of which he is the President, bring together frequently under his roof the most gifted and accomplished residents and visitors at the capital. He likes a game of whist, tells and enjoys a good joke or story, and when the tension of work or study is relaxed, he devotes himself to recreation with the zest of a man still warmed by the impulses of youth.

He has little or nothing of the instinct of money-getting, and the two homes above alluded to represent the aggregate savings of his busy life. As a lawyer he could have amassed a fortune in a few years ; had he been less than the scrupulously honest man that he is, his opportunities as the custodian of immense public interests might have indirectly yielded him a competence ; but as it is he is content, and, in comparison with his other gifts, poor in purse. His hospitality is proverbial. He is never so happy as when his house and table are filled with genial friends. A dinner or a family break-fast with him is an opportunity never to be missed, for the latest good book, the newest thing in art, or politics, or literature are sure to come up for an airing before the meal is over. He not only talks well, but he has that even greater and rarer faculty of putting other people at their best and helping them to tell what they know better than they have ever said it before. None of his successes in later life have made him for-getful of the friends who were true to him in his earlier years, and a class-mate, a veteran soldier of the Forty-Second Regiment, or an old neighbour who knew him when the "Widow Garfield's boy" taught school or worked on the neighbouring farms, is sure of as cordial a greeting as a Cabinet Minister.

He is not an intense partisan, and some of the thorniest places in his political path have been where he has taken too broad and im-partial a view of pending questions to suit the views and purposes of other party leaders; but he is a republican of that consistent, symmetrical type which recognizes in the people a great, watchful, powerful sovereign, whose patriotism, intelligence, and readiness to make any necessary sacrifice for the common good may always be implicitly trusted. His religion is of that practical, every day quality which gives a tone of purity and moral strength to his life ; he is a Christian without cant, a worshipper without hypocrisy.

It has been the good fortune of General Garfield to enjoy a domestic life of unclouded sunshine. At the Geauga Seminary, when sixteen years of age, he met a quiet, studious, intellectual girl, named Lucretia Rudolph, between whom and himself there was kindled an attachment which years afterwards ripened into a betrothal, and they were married at Hiram shortly after his graduation at Williams' College. Four sons and one daughter have blessed that felicitous marriage, and perhaps the saddest day the family has known was when the two elder boys were separated from the home-nest and sent away to College. The honoured mother of President Garfield still lives, a bright, cheerful, venerable old lady, to share his home and see the ripe fruition of the life for which she toiled and prayed in the days of her early widowhood. Neither she nor any of the family have been, in any sense, elated by the events of the past year, which have made her son the first man in American history who has been at the same time Representative, Senator, and President-Elect of the United States.

And thus, blest in his family surroundings, honoured by his countrymen, trained by experience in State affairs as no previous President has been prepared for the Executive office, General Garfield goes from his farm-house at Mentor to the Chair of State consecrated by Washington. His administration begins at a time when the country is prosperous, confident of its future, and at peace with all the world. The new Executive illustrates in his own attainments and career the priceless value of that freedom of opportunity, which is the heritage of youth and manhood under " a government of the people by the people, for the people." The whole record of his past life carries the assurance that he will honour his great opportunity, and leave behind him when he retires an administration worthy of the best years of the Republic.

BASLE, *March*, 1881.

END.

PRINTED BY BALLANTYNE, HANSON AND CO.
LONDON AND EDINBURGH

www.ingramcontent.com/pod-product-compliance
Lightning Source LLC
Chambersburg PA
CBHW020752020726
47495CB00008B/2392